· TALES FROM SCHROON LAKE ·

Hobo Holiday

WRITTEN BY

Barbara Davoll

Pictures by Dennis Hockerman

MOODY

To Jack Wyrtzen, encourager and fellow-laborer in the gospel, whose consistent, godly life and ministry at Word of Life International has written the real *"Tales from Schroon Lake"* and has brought our little dot on the map to the attention of the world.

"This book of the law shall not depart out of thy mouth, but thou shalt meditate therein day and night, that thou mayest observe to do according to all that is written therein; for then thou shalt make thy way prosperous, and then thou shalt have good success."

Joshua 1:8

Moody Press, a ministry of the Moody Bible Institute, is designed for education, evangelization, and edification. If we may assist you in knowing more about Christ and the Christian life, please write us without obligation: Moody Press, c/o MLM, Chicago, IL 60610.

ISBN: 0-8024-1033-2
13579108642
Printed in the United States of America

"Tales From Schroon Lake," is the newest animal adventure series for children written by Barbara Davoll. It takes its setting from the tiny town of Schroon Lake, high in the Adirondack Mountains of upstate New York, where Barbara and her husband, Roy, make their home and serve the Lord with Word of Life International as Children's Representatives. The Davolls are lovingly known around the world as "Uncle Roy and Aunt Barb" as they minister in children's crusades at home and abroad.

Barbara is well known for her award-winning, best-selling Christopher Churchmouse Classics and the Molehole Mystery series. She has allowed her many talents and abilities to be used for the Lord in the areas of writing, composing, teaching, and music, but she loves being a wife, mother, and grandmother and still enjoys being a homemaker for Roy and their schnauzer, Josh.

Illustrator Dennis Hockerman collaborated with friend Barbara Davoll to bring to life a family of lovable churchmice, a captivating underground village of moles, and now a charming band of beavers. Balancing fun-filled imagery with the natural realism of life in a beaver lodge proved to be a real challenge in creating the "Tales From Schroon Lake" series. The artist enjoys viewing the world through a child's eyes and works almost exclusively in the children's market. He lives with his wife, three children, and two Yorkshire terriers in Mequon, Wisconsin, a Milwaukee suburb.

It was a cold, crisp night in late fall. A big yellow moon climbed high in the sky above the mountains in the North Country. CRASH! A huge tree fell into the lake with a splash. Bucky Beaver and his family were hard at work building a winter lodge. It would be their new home.

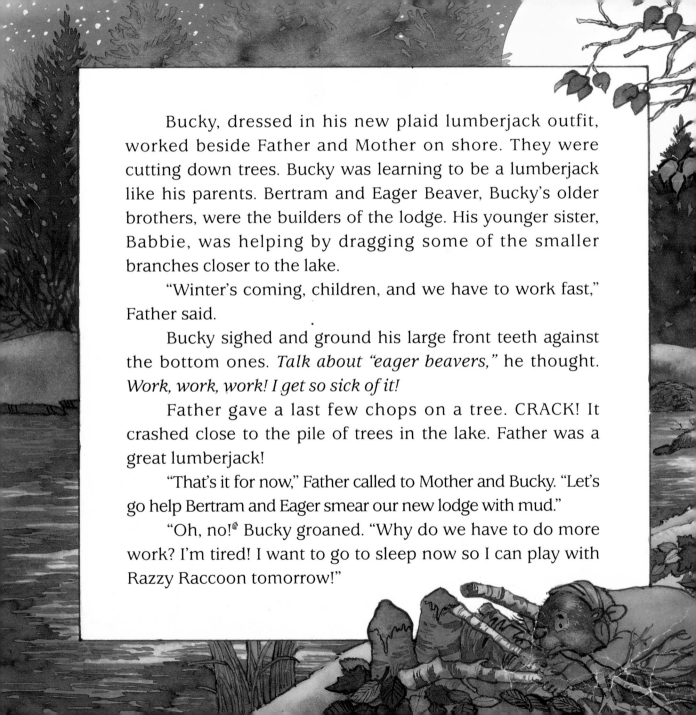

Bucky, dressed in his new plaid lumberjack outfit, worked beside Father and Mother on shore. They were cutting down trees. Bucky was learning to be a lumberjack like his parents. Bertram and Eager Beaver, Bucky's older brothers, were the builders of the lodge. His younger sister, Babbie, was helping by dragging some of the smaller branches closer to the lake.

"Winter's coming, children, and we have to work fast," Father said.

Bucky sighed and ground his large front teeth against the bottom ones. *Talk about "eager beavers,"* he thought. *Work, work, work! I get so sick of it!*

Father gave a last few chops on a tree. CRACK! It crashed close to the pile of trees in the lake. Father was a great lumberjack!

"That's it for now," Father called to Mother and Bucky. "Let's go help Bertram and Eager smear our new lodge with mud."

"Oh, no!" Bucky groaned. "Why do we have to do more work? I'm tired! I want to go to sleep now so I can play with Razzy Raccoon tomorrow!"

"You can play with Razzy," Mother said. "But we need to get our home finished now. Come on, Bucky. Let's go help."

I wish I were a raccoon like Razzy, Bucky thought. He followed his parents under the water to get mud for their new home. *Beavers never have time for fun. There has to be a better way to live than working all the time.*

Early the next morning Bucky swam across the lake toward Razzy's home. As soon as he was on shore he thumped his tail three times. That was a special signal that all the beaver world understood. But Bucky had found it was also a good way to call Razzy. In a few minutes he heard his friend's cheerful voice.

"Hi, Buck! Glad you came! I've got something to show you," said Razzy. "Follow me!"

The raccoon took off like a shot through the woods. Bucky puffed after him. After a time they came out of the woods on the other side of the lake.

"There!" Razzy said, pointing. "Do you see them?"

Bucky's eyes grew wide, and he drew in his breath. Two men were sitting by a fire built on the ground.

"Let's get out of here, Razz. Men are dangerous! They kill beavers," he said fearfully. "My dad said not to go near men. You can't trust them."

"Not these men, Bucky," Razzy laughed. "They are hoboes."

Bucky stared at the men sitting by the fire. "What–what are hoboes?"

"Nothing to be scared of, silly," Razzy laughed. "This kind of hobo just lies around all day doing nothing. What a life they have!"

Bucky breathed a little easier. The men did seem harmless, and he didn't see guns anywhere. As he watched, one man walked down to the water.

"Watch him, now," said Razzy. "I've been watching them for days. He's going to fish."

The animals watched as the hobo tied a string around his finger and lazily threw it into the water. Then the man lay down on the beach and pulled his hat over his eyes.

"See! When he gets a fish, the string will wiggle his finger. He'll just take a nap till he catches one," the raccoon said. "He's really smart!"

"Yeah," agreed the beaver. "Where's their house?"

"They don't have one," the coon said with a giggle. "They live right out in the open. Isn't that great?"

Bucky laughed, thinking of men living like that. "No wonder they don't have to work," he said. "Beavers have to build lodges and dams and store food for winter."

That evening after supper, Bucky told his father about the hoboes.

"Why can't we be like them?" he asked. "I don't like to work."

Bucky's father sat up straight in his chair and got a shocked look on his face. "Why, Son, those men usually beg from others for a living instead of working."

"But Father, they were fishing. Isn't that work?"

"Not the way they do it," argued his father. "I'm surprised that you would waste your time watching them."

Bucky swallowed hard. "Father—I—I would like to—to join them. I mean—live like they do."

The expression on his father's face was almost more than the little beaver could stand. Mother Beaver laid aside her knitting and looked very worried. Babbie sat staring at her brother in surprise.

"Oh, Bucky, you wouldn't want to leave home, would you?" she asked.

"I'd like to try it," he answered. "I think I'm old enough, and it would be fun. Could I, please, Father?"

Father Beaver looked at his son. "All right, Bucky," Father agreed slowly. "But I really don't think it is best."

Bucky began to dance around the lodge. Then he ran to his room to pack. He tied a few favorite things in a big red cloth and ran back into the living room. His family stood waiting to tell him good-bye.

Mother looked at her youngest son, with tears in her eyes. "You know the beaver signal, Son," she said. "Just thump three times if you need help. We'll be right there—if—if we can," she finished tearfully.

Bucky knew he had to go right away or he would change his mind. He gave his parents a final hug and quickly left the beaver lodge.

He decided to swim to the hobo camp. When he saw the tiny light of their fire, he swam toward shore and entered the woods. Creeping close, he could hear them talking.

"You have to catch more fish than this, Henry. This one is hardly a bite for me," said one of them.

"Then you'd better catch your own, Jake. I didn't expect to share it with you anyway."

"Too much work," Jake yawned. "I'll just go to sleep so I won't notice how hungry I am." Jake stumbled away from the fire, lay down on the ground, and used his arm for a pillow.

Bucky watched from behind a tree. *I guess I should go to sleep too,* he thought. He tried to make himself comfortable. "Ouch!" he cried as a stick poked him in the ribs. *This sure isn't as comfortable as my bed at home.*

The night sounds of the forest frightened him. A twig snapped in the woods nearby, and Bucky jumped. He was afraid, and the cold mountain air had chilled him to the bone.

Bucky didn't see a large, furry animal move behind the tree close to where he was lying and watch him silently.

The beaver turned over fitfully, trying to get some rest. But sleep would not come. *This night is much too long and noisy, he thought.*

As morning came to the north woods, Bucky heard angry sounds coming from the hobo camp.

"That's my can of beans," yelled Jake at Henry. "Keep your hands off!"

"You tried to eat my fish," snarled Henry.

Jake jumped up and raised his fists.

"Cut it out, you two," growled a gruff-looking man Bucky had not seen before. He had a thick black beard. His hair looked as if it had never seen a comb. "You guys make me sick, always fighting," he complained.

"Well, you make *us* sick too," responded Henry. "You smell like a skunk! You haven't had a bath for a year."

Bucky clapped his paw over his mouth. Some of his best friends were skunks. He had never noticed their having a bad odor.

"Yeah? Well, you guys aren't petunias either," snapped the big, gruff man.

"I'm going fishing," stormed Henry. Angrily he stomped away from the campsite.

"Don't bother! You don't catch enough to keep an ant alive," Jake yelled.

Henry headed for the water, untangling his mess of fishing string from his pocket.

Suddenly a cold wind whistled through the hoboes' camp. It sent leaves flying all around Bucky. *Father was right*, thought the beaver, shuddering. *Winter is on its way. Those look like snow clouds.*

The hoboes began to stir up their fire.

"Looks like a bad storm coming, Jake," said Henry, rushing back to the fire.

"Yeah, and us with no food. What are we going to do?"

"We're not going to eat fish, that's for sure," answered Henry. "They're not biting. Too cold." He shivered.

Oh no! thought Bucky. *What will I eat? I'm getting hungry already.*

There were many trees around that a beaver could eat, but they were all out in the open. He was afraid the hoboes would see him. Suddenly Bucky felt something hit his nose. Large flakes of snow were beginning to fall from the gray sky. Bucky knew he had to find food and shelter fast.

The hoboes can be lazy if they want, he said to himself, *but I think it's better to work than starve or freeze.* Bucky made a frantic dash for a tree and began to chomp on it. He knew the hoboes must have seen him.

"Quick, Henry, it's a beaver!" he heard Jake yell. "Get him. We can sell his fur!"

Bucky stopped chewing and ran for the woods. The hoboes were right behind him, crashing through the leaves and twigs. Bucky's legs were short, and his body was heavy. They would catch him for sure.

Just then he spotted a fallen tree. There was a small space between its branches and the ground. Perhaps he could hide there if they didn't see him.

As Bucky tried to hide, he realized his body was too big for the narrow opening between the tree and the ground. There was no room for his legs. Frantically he tried to pull them in under him. But he was not in time. Jake was close behind him.

As Jake jumped over the tree he stepped right on Bucky's leg. Snap went the bone in his leg. Bucky bit his tongue to keep from screaming.

Jake kept right on going. He didn't know he had broken Bucky's leg. He had not seen the beaver. Neither had his hobo friends.

"Let him go," yelled Henry, who was farther behind. "He'll probably die in the storm. Then we can just get the fur. That will be easier than chasing him."

They're right, thought Bucky, with hot tears falling. The pain from his leg was almost unbearable. He moaned. *I will die with no one to help me. I can't run, and soon the snow will be deep. Oh, why did I ever leave my wonderful family?*

Bucky was so jammed under the tree he could hardly move. There wasn't room for him to thump his tail for help, and the pain from his leg was terrible. It was beginning to grow dark in the woods as the snow came down. He groaned to himself. *This is the end. No one will ever know where I am.*

It was so foolish of me to think I could live without working. Look at the hoboes, he thought. *They have no food or shelter. I should have been smarter than that.*

Tears froze on his fur. Hours passed, as the snow fell silently. Bucky and the tree were covered with snow.

Bucky was nearly frozen when a dark shadow fell across the opening of his hiding place. *Oh, no! The hoboes have found me!* thought Bucky in fear.

"Bucky? Are you there?" whispered a familiar voice.

"Father! Is that you?" cried the frantic little beaver.

"Shhh!" warned his father. "The hoboes will hear us. Come on out if you can." Father lifted some of the branches, and painfully Bucky pulled himself out from under the tree. His leg hurt so badly he could hardly move.

"Oh, Son, are you all right?" asked his anxious father, bending over him.

"I—I think so," sobbed Bucky quietly. "But they broke my leg."

"I know," his father said sadly. "I saw it happen."

"You did?" whispered his son. "Where were you?"

"I was right here in the woods where I've been all along. I followed you, Son, in case you got into trouble and needed me."

So that was what I heard in the woods, thought Bucky. His heart melted at the thought of his loving father watching over him.

"Now we must go," Father said urgently. "I'll have to carry you through the woods. We won't be able to swim, since your leg is injured."

Bucky nodded, with tears running down his face. It would be so hard for Father to carry him in the snow.

The father beaver picked up his son and began to trudge through the snow. It was a long, hard trip home.

The next day Bucky lay propped up in bed. His broken leg was neatly bandaged. Mother sat beside him, spooning birchbark soup into his mouth. Bertram, Eager and Babbie played quietly nearby. Father watched lovingly from the foot of the bed.

"Father," said Bucky weakly, "I was so wrong. Those hoboes have a terrible life. They don't have any place to get in out of the cold, and they are hungry. They fight all the time."

"I know, Son. Remember, I tried to tell you," answered Father. "But there are some lessons that can only be learned the hard way. A beaver would be miserable all of his life if he didn't do something useful. We were created to work."

"Working is a lot easier than the hoboes' life," said Bucky thoughtfully.

"That's true, Bucky dear," Mother agreed, as she finished feeding him the bark soup.

"Those poor hoboes don't have a wonderful family like mine. How long will it take for my leg to heal?" he asked.

"I'm afraid it will take months," replied Father. "You won't be able to swim or go out until next spring."

Bucky groaned. "It was sure dumb of me," he said gloomily. "What will I do while all of you work outside?"

"Oh, you can always do things for Mom," laughed Bertram.

"Why, of course," said Mother sweetly, giving him a spoonful of lovely bark pudding. "I can keep him 'busy as a beaver.'"

They all laughed as Bucky slurped another spoonful of pudding. His Hobo Holiday was over. But he would always remember the lessons he had learned.